Advanc

"Happy Ty

T0090601

"Bob Nozik has created a wonderful book of poetry with great humor that gives us the keys to a happy life. I love this book, I will confess. Just take a look, for your success! Bob has written a clever and funny book, but most importantly, he helps you to laugh, especially with yourself. Rabindranath Tagore said:'The progress of our soul is like a perfect poem. It has an infinite idea which once realized makes all movements full of meaning and joy.' *Happy Tymes Rhymes* is the perfect poetic progress your soul has yearned for. Great meaning and joy await you, since each poem is a pearl of brilliance."

—**Lionel Ketchian,** *Founder of Happiness Clubs International*

✳ ✳ ✳

"Bob Nozik crystallizes his concepts and illuminates these 12 principles with poetic precision!"

—**Lenny Dave,** *President of AATH—Association for Applied & Therapeutic Humor*

✳ ✳ ✳

"One of the great things about rhymes is that, when done well, just a few words can clearly convey deep and complex thoughts, ideas and emotions in a way that seems effortless.

In *Happy Tymes Rhymes*, Bob Nozik does exactly that. With a delightfully playful style that matches the tone of his book (*Happy 4 Life: Here's How to Do It*) these rhymes, cleverly and succinctly explain each of his twelve keys to happiness.

This is an amazing book that illustrates Bob's knowledge of what constitutes true happiness in a way that will be easily understood by anyone!"

—**David Ambrose,** *creator of the Happiness Minute*

✳ ✳ ✳

"Written by a man who has mastered sustainable happiness, the poems in this book offer a wealth of insight into how to live a truly happy life. Dr. Bob Nozik's wisdom in happiness is as good as gold and I trust you will find the answers to your questions about the elusive topic of happiness right here in a witty and entertaining fashion."

—**Aymee Coget,** *Ph. D., Speaker, writer and teacher of happiness*

Happy Tymes Rhymes

Just for the Fun of It

By

Bob Nozik, MD

Order this book online at www.trafford.com
or email orders@trafford.com

Most Trafford titles are also available at major online book retailers.

Note for Librarians: A cataloguing record for this book is available from Library
and Archives Canada at www.collectionscanada.ca/amicus/index-e.html

Printed in Victoria, BC, Canada.

ISBN: 978-1-4269-0289-5 (Soft)

*Our mission is to efficiently provide the world's finest, most comprehensive
book publishing service, enabling every author to experience success.
To find out how to publish your book, your way, and have it available
worldwide, visit us online at www.trafford.com*

Trafford rev. 8/26/2009

 www.trafford.com

North America & international
toll-free: 1 888 232 4444 (USA & Canada)
phone: 250 383 6864 ◆ fax: 812 355 4082

Table of Contents

Acknowledgments

I want to thank Grant Flint for his encouragement, general critique, editorial and content contributions to this work; Kevin Coffey for the original drawings; Tiffany Colby for the cover photo; Joe Sikoryak for technical and artistic advice; and most of all, Marsha and Jillian for their love, support, critique, and encouragement throughout.

Introduction

A collection of rhyming poems? Where is Dr. Seuss when you need him? We know happiness is important, perhaps the most treasured, most desired quality to which the human animal aspires. And after more than two millennia of fruitless searching, we may now, at last, be moving to within hailing distance of true happiness. You notice, I just qualified happiness with the adjective, "true," for happiness is one of the most common emotions that, along with sadness, anger, and unhappiness, we humans experience. But the emotion of happiness is not the true, lasting, abiding, all-consuming happiness humans since the time of Aristotle, have sought. The emotion of happiness, as the new science of happiness is quick to point out, is fleeting; a temporary, ephemeral touch, a peck on the cheek, a passing hint of what the happiness of our dreams could be. What we really crave is happiness as a Way of Living; happiness that won't abandon us at the first hint of trouble; happiness we can count on to be there for us through life's inevitable twists and turns. We want to BE happiness, not just sample brief tastes of the precious stuff; we want a sturdy happiness not held hostage by the vagaries of capricious circumstance.

The ancient Greeks understood this better, it seems, than we. They labeled the common, fleeting, kiss of happiness "Hedonic happiness," those delicious interludes of joyous explosion and pleasure that were never meant to be more than temporary responses to good fortune, certainly not the basis for a happy life.

There is another happiness which is much more than an emotional response to sensual pleasure or good fortune. This, the Greeks called, 'Eudaimonic happiness,' happiness we generate ourselves from down deep within us. This happiness, which a lucky few enjoy simply because they were genetically favored, the rest of us have to earn. By cultivating certain inner qualities like gratitude, self-esteem, non-judgment, and others, we can transform our lives from ordinary to exceptional. We all can, by consciously recreating our inner make up, live lives of constantly elevating, inner contentment and joy EVERY MOMENT OF OUR LIVES.

This little book of rhyming poetry is a start. These poems take their inspiration from the immortal Dr. Seuss in being fun to read but packed with wisdom. Because of the fun, they will appeal to children. But don't be fooled; their instructions for how to live life with happiness could not be more momentous for everyone, young and old. The poems in this collection are companion pieces to my book, Happy 4 Life: Here's How to Do It. (Trafford, 2004, Vancouver, B. C., Canada)

Because I have dedicated my life to helping everyone become happier than they ever thought possible, I have included my email address below and encourage anyone with questions about how to live a happy life, to contact me.

Meanwhile, enjoy the poems for the confections that they are, but don't neglect the insights mixed in with the merriment.

Bob Nozik, MD
PollyannaN@aol.com

Happy
Tymes
Rhymes

"om, omm, ommm"

Conscious Awareness

All twelve happiness keys are important, but if I were pressed to name one I consider the most important, it would be conscious awareness. It is hard to imagine someone not manifesting abiding happiness whose conscious awareness was well developed, especially in its highest forms: attention and the connection to the soul and the spirit. This happiness key, along with Perfection, unites happiness with spirituality and religion. And while it is possible to be deeply happy without being religious or spiritual, it is undeniable that joining with our higher selves helps immensely.

Only after I completed all of these poems did I notice that each of them takes a similar format. All are composed of 14 verses and, by and large, the first seven establish the problem while the last seven respond to, or solve, the problem.

This poem concerns someone beaten down by practical, everyday problems and who needs to know that there is a larger view recognized by our Higher Self.

Conscious Awareness

I know myself
       I'm what I do,
My hobbies, job,
       My family too.

I live my life,
       I fight the fights,
I smell, touch, taste,
       Hear sounds, see sights.

The world is made
       Of concrete stuff,
To claim it's not
       Is foolish fluff.

We're born and schooled,
       Have kids and work,
Retiring late,
       Our only perk.

Is this our best
       And only fate,
To breed and work,
       To fight and hate?

With all hope gone,
       No special twist,
I'm just a sad
       Existentialist.

But Buddha, Christ,
       Mohammed say,
"Don't sell out short,
       You've lost your way."

"Extend your sense,
        Accept the dare,
Expand your thirst
        To be aware.

"And focus too,
        There's power there,
Convergent force
        Will bring to bear."

"But you're much more
        Than sensing beast,
Your sacred Soul,
        An endless feast.

"To Higher Self
        You should relate,
To search and find,
        Just meditate.

"And as you move
        Far past your form,
All limits lift,
        Beyond the storm

"Your Spirit is
        The real You,
Expand your sight,
        Enlarge your view.

"We're Gods, not men,
        Nor simple beast,
Be all you are
        Enjoy the feast!"

"I LOVE ME SOOOO MUCH!"

SELF-LIKE/LOVE

Most folks, I've observed, seem to take an odd delight in putting themselves down. They criticize practically everything about themselves, seeming to almost hope that in so doing, others might try and talk them out of it. What this creates is an tidal-wave of self-styled misery and dislike of self. Much of this self-generated carping originates from those voices inside our heads commonly called the "Inner-Critic." Many of us have severe, angry, parental voices that are insulting, disrespectful, and rude. But they've been there since we were little and we've grown so accustomed to them that we seem not to realize the damage they do to our feelings of self-love and respect.

If we truly are to live happy lives, we must terminate our critics' reign of terror. We need to convert these harsh inner-critics from petty dictators into what I like to call respectful, empathetic inner-colleagues. That is the message of this poem.

Self-Like/Love

We're with ourselves
        Both night and day,
No way, in fact
        To get away.

Some folks I know
        Would, if they could,
Divorce themselves
        And leave for good.

And with great glee
        They criticize
Their moral values
        And their thighs.

Their inner voice
        Their critic's muse,
With words and taunts,
        Themselves abuse.

The point, I guess,
        Is to complain,
They hope to get
        A better brain.

I guess I'll have to
        Be the one
To show them how
        To have more fun.

It's simple, really,
        Not so hard,
Your inner critic
        Must be barred.

You do your best,
        You always try,
You mean no harm
        Not girl or guy.

You're all you've got
        And that ain't bad,
So dump the critic,
        Who makes you sad.

You're with yourself
        Twenty four/seven,
So turn your life
        Into your heaven.

It's time, I say,
        To make a friend,
Past time, I say,
        Self hate must end.

The who you are
        Is all you need,
Best friends become
        And you'll succeed.

The love you seek
        Must first be you,
For happiness
        Both deep and true.

So with yourself
        As friend and lover,
The joy you lost
        You will recover.

Self-Esteem

Low self-esteem is at the root of much of the unhappiness in the world today. Contrary to what many people believe, self-esteem has more to do with how you feel about what you do than with your ability to do good work itself. There are many talented people who perform on a high level but still suffer from low self-esteem. Don't be taken in by those who, as many prominent sports stars, loudly proclaim their own greatness. Insisting that others kowtow to their matchless prowess is the wall of pseudo self-esteem behind which those with low self-esteem hide. As was the case with self-like, a severe inner-critic is the chief culprit fueling low self-esteem.

A simple way for evaluating your self-esteem is asking how proud you are of yourself. With good self-esteem, we know that we will do whatever is asked of us to the best of our ability and responsibly. That really is all that is needed for high self-esteem.

Self-Esteem

I'm very smart,
      So I've been told,
But that refrain
      Is getting old.

Deep down inside
      I feel no good
I can't do what
      I think I should.

At work I hide,
      "Choose him instead."
I can't compete,
      My brain is dead.

The boss, with evil
      Grin confides:
"This one is yours."
      He softly chides.

I work all day
      And evenings too,
Amazingly,
      I see it through.

"Good work, m'boy,
      I knew you could."
I smile but think,
      "I'm still no good."

Sometimes, inside,
      I want to scream,
It's hard to have
      Low self-esteem.

Your inner critic
        Is to blame,
The lies it feeds
        You must disclaim.

You only need
        To do your best.
Do that, my friend,
        And you'll be blessed.

And run your critic
        Out the door,
Insults from him
        You'll need no more.

You know your strengths,
        It's what you've got.
Believe! Embrace!
        Use them a lot.

We all have weak spots,
        Don't despair.
With them just use
        Some extra care.

Enjoy the person
        That you are,
Enjoy your gifts,
        That's not bizarre.

You can live life
        With self-esteem,
You can enjoy
        Your fondest dream.

"THANK YOU, THANK YOU, THANK YOU!"

Appreciation/ Gratitude

Many of us stumble through life wearing blinders; not physical blinders, but psychological ones. These are much more impenetrable than physical ones. Appreciation is the intake; we need to raise our heads and behold the wonders that envelop us moment by moment, every day of our lives. Gratitude is our output; an outpouring of thanks for the gift of life in this amazing world. Sadly, for many of us, it is only when we are poised to exit life that we begin noticing and appreciating what before we had taken for granted.

Gratitude (along with appreciation) is a happiness key that is recognized and valued by everyone involved in happiness work. Make it a habit to notice even the small wonders of the world every day and your happiness will blossom.

Appreciation/Gratitude

He trudges forward,
     Slow and steady,
His burden huge
     So dark and leady.

His blinders keep
     Him on the road,
He sees just gravel,
     Feels his load.

He goes this way
     From nine to five,
It's what he does
     To be alive.

This beast of burden's
     Not a steed,
Nor ox nor bull
     Too dumb to read.

This tethered soul
     Is you and me,
We've chosen how
     To not be free.

The beauty that
     Surrounds us all,
All winter, summer,
     Spring and fall,

We choose to live
     With blinders set,
We choose a life
     Filled with regret.

A world of splendor
        All around,
Trees, mountains, birds,
        There to be found.

And life itself
        In all its wonder,
A miracle
        Beyond all other.

We have to work
        And learn to hate,
To lose the awe
        The gods create.

Cast off your blinders,
        Dark and rude,
And fill your heart
        With gratitude.

You're not in prison,
        Chained or dead,
You're light in motion,
        Raise up your head.

Your life is love,
        It's what you are,
Cast off that anchor,
        You are a star.

Your life is now,
        No need to wait,
The world is yours,
        Appreciate!

"OH WELL. ACCIDENTS HAPPEN!"

Acceptance

Leading a happy life does not require that we pretend there are no ills in the world. There is pain, real pain. There is death, disease, misery, sadness, cruelty, and suffering. Being truly happy asks only that we face life's downsides honestly and courageously. The Serenity Prayer has within it everything necessary for us to live happily even in the face of life's tough stuff.

The Serenity Prayer

God grant me the serenity
To accept the things I cannot change,
The courage to change the things I can,
And the wisdom to know the difference.

This insightful poem addresses the pain we all face, but in a way that is compatible with enduring happiness. Happy people know there is pain and suffering in the world which they must confront and deal with. Acceptance is the way to do that while still remaining happy.

Acceptance

The pain of life
    Is just too much
It pulls me down,
    I'm numb to touch.

A loved one dies,
    A deal falls through,
I lose my job,
    The rent is due.

The earth gets hot,
    The oceans rise,
Tsunami hits,
    A mother cries.

It's just not right,
    It's wrong, in fact,
For happy times
    Must be an act.

And yet, my wise
    And happy friend,
The shouts of doom,
    They never end.

Your secret, please,
    I need to know,
Out of my grief
    I want to go.

So tell me now,
    No, tell us all,
How we can rise
    Above the pall.

The Yoda Master
        Sets his stare,
"You've heard, of course,
        The Serenity Prayer?

"Accept those things
        You cannot change,
This simple task
        You must arrange.

"You needn't like
        The nasty stuff,
Accepting it
        Is good enough.

"That lifts you up
        To work for good,
To make things right
        With what you could.

"Your happiness
        Will keep you strong
To fight the fight,
        To right the wrong.

"So just be wise
        And pick your fight,
Accept what's done
        And right the right."

With that, he smiled
        His Yoda smile,
This truth he told
        Would last a while.

Responsible Adulthood

Insisting that we live as responsible adults sounds so, well, grown up, mature, not any fun at all. But, in fact, being responsible and fully adult unlocks freedom's door, permitting us to travel far beyond the limited course open to those who are childish and irresponsible. Simply knowing that we will be responsible in our actions means we can be free to try more, be more adventurous, but in a way that will harm no one, not others nor ourselves. This is real freedom. And being adult, in the best sense of the word, frees us to test and stretch our limits to the fullest. This is the guilt-free life we covet and can enjoy once we know we are looking out for ourselves and anyone and anything else our actions might affect.

Responsible Adulthood

A clever child
     Without much stress
Learns to play
     And make a mess.

Asks someone big,
     Like Mom or Dad,
They'll clean stuff up
     And not be mad.

"He's just a kid,
     He's not to blame.
It's how they play,
     It's just their game."

What's good for kids,
     Age six to eight,
When they grow up,
     Does not translate.

When things go wrong
     In adult life,
It doesn't work
     To blame your wife.

To be grown up
     And credible,
We need to be
     Responsible.

The adult child,
     Avoiding fault,
Blames others for
     His bad result.

This faulty logic
        Has a cost,
His life's command
        Is sadly lost.

Those others that
        Control his fate,
He fears and even
        Learns to hate.

But foolish, foolish,
        Grown up child,
Take back the life
        That you exiled.

You are in charge,
        Not Mom or Dad,
Nor boss nor friend,
        For that be glad!

You must be master
        Of your ship.
You chart the course
        Of every trip.

The payoff's big
        For those who do,
Their happiness
        Runs deep and true.

So leave the child,
        For that day's done,
It's time you had
        Your grown up fun.

"BAD! DISGUSTING! JUST PLAIN WRONG!"

Non-Judgment

Many of us succumb to the trap of being judgmental; it is so seductive that few are able to resist its clarion call. But being judgmental is a poison-pill trap ushering us into a life of disappointment and unhappiness. Judgment is polarizing, recognizing only black and white, right and wrong. Yet life is not that way. Life is filled with nuance and shades of grey. Rarely is there anything in life that is all good or bad, and acknowledging this gives life its delightful complexity. In judging, we compare life to an arbitrary standard in which only one of the myriad ways life presents can be right; all the other ways must then be judged negatively. Therefore, of necessity, the judge always makes many more negative judgments than positive. Generating negative judgments over and over pulls negative emotions in with them making it almost impossible for judgmental people to be happy.

Non-Judgment

I am the judge
  Of my domain.
"He's bad! She's wrong!
  And you're insane!"

I judge a lot
  Because I can.
I judge the world.
  I am the man!

The judge, of course,
  Decides what's right.
He's strong and quick,
  He's very bright.

But judges lead
  A troubled life,
Their judgments cause
  A lot of strife.

The world is not
  All black and white.
It's shades of grey
  That get it right.

The judge finds few
  Who pass their test,
They fail despite
  Their very best.

"It wears me out,
  So much that's bad,
To judge all day
  Just makes me mad."

Non judgment is
  The better way,
For peace of mind,
  It's here to stay.

It also fits
  The facts we know
For how things work
  And how things go.

Few things in life
  Are absolute,
And judging life
  Will cause dispute.

So judge me not
  Lest I judge you,
We'd both be harmed
  And neither true.

The happy way
  Is not so hard,
When judgment tempts
  It should be barred.

Let life and people
  Have their way,
Just watch and learn,
  You'll have your day.

Enjoy what's here
  Allow the game,
No need to rule,
  No need to blame.

"OH GOOD— SHE WOULDN'T BE SO ANGRY IF SHE DIDN'T LOVE ME! "

Pollyanna's Game

Nowadays, Pollyanna is a name we hear used pejoratively;
"Don't be such a Pollyanna!", the implied accusation is that we are being too happy, inappropriately happy. But Pollyanna got a bad rap. Using what we've just learned about judgment, we understand that if we but look, there are things we can legitimately like even in those things usually called bad. This is the basis of Pollyanna's Game, one of the most powerful instruments in our happiness tool bag. The "Just be glad game," to use Pollyanna's original phraseology, asks us to dig deeper into the small, everyday bad stuff that happens in our lives: things like knocking over a glass of water or getting a flat tire. The Game instructs us to look for the hidden gifts in what is commonly called bad. And when we do, amazingly, we always find things there we can truly like. "What good luck! It's just a water-spill, no one hurt, nothing stained." "So glad we've got AAA and a cell phone to call for help."

Transforming the just be glad game into a habit by using it over and over is one of the best ways for jet-starting your path to deep, inner happiness.

Pollyanna's Game

"The Game," she said,
    "Is just be glad.
Most things in life
    Are not all bad."

"The stuff we like,
    No problem there,
My fun and games,
    Your perfect hair."

But what about
    The other stuff,
This leaking pipe,
    That steak too tough?

For life, I'm sure
    You will agree,
It's not all toast
    With jam and tea.

Those little things
    That pull us down:
Spaghetti stains
    On ballroom gown.

The traffic's bad,
    The air not clean,
The moldy cheese
    All dry and green.

Throughout each day
    And Sundays too
It wears me out
    I tell you true.

"The trick" she cries
        "Is digging deep
At what at first
        Would make you weep."

"Some good to find
        In what's called bad,
Pray look again
        And don't get mad."

We tend to see
        Just black and white,
But life is more
        Then wrong and right.

There's bad in good
        And good in bad,
This gives us hope
        For what's called sad.

The Game is not
        A silly move,
The joy you get
        You will approve.

And habit forming
        Is this Game,
For happiness
        You will soon tame.

So Pollyanna
        Young and smart,
Teach us your Game
        Of fact and art.

Handling Mistakes

Making mistakes is the primary way we learn life's lessons.
Yet, most of us detest making mistakes. We'll deny, shift blame, accuse, and if nothing else works, damn the fickle fate that brought us the mistake. While no one likes making mistakes, we need to embrace the priceless teaching mistakes bring with them. It is by learning through our mistakes that we grow in wisdom and grace as the years roll by.

So, fear not; step boldly into the world. Try things out and deal with your inevitable failures responsibly and honestly, understanding that the knowledge gleaned from those mistakes will transform into pure gold for your ultimate effectiveness and happiness in life.

Handling Mistakes

Mistakes it seems
    Are part of me,
I've always made them,
    Two or three

I'd make a plan
    And try it out,
I'm smart you see
    Without a doubt.

Sometimes I'd win,
    Sometimes I'd lose,
But either way
    Some would accuse.

They'd stand and say,
    With feet spread wide,
With frown and scowl
    And even pride:

"A terrible thing
    You've gone and done,
Mistakes, mistakes,
    You've made, my son.

"You're wrong again
    You've blundered bad,
The mess you've made
    Should make you sad."

I frown and look
    Down at my feet
For what I've done,
    Accept defeat.

But still and all
     It seems to me
Mistakes done right
     Can set us free.

In life's great lab
     We try things out,
Life teaches us,
     Without a doubt.

When plans turn out
     It shows we knew,
It proves our point
     No need to stew.

But when we're wrong,
     A big mistake,
New lessons learned
     Back home to take.

Clean up the mess
     Do what you need
So no one suffers
     From your deed.

Then celebrate,
     You win the prize,
For what you've got
     Can make you wise.

So make mistakes,
     Don't be afraid,
And what you learn
     Is how you're paid.

Individuality

So, who are you...really? Do you even know? Most of us have been so molded and shaped, folded and spindled from the time we were born that we have no idea who we are. This cookie-cutter upbringing can cost us our unique genius, those special skills and qualities that set us apart.

Not knowing who we really are leads us to struggle with low self-esteem and lack of self-love. Without self-knowledge, how can we trust ourselves to drive our own bus, direct our lives? In ignorance of whom we truly are, it seems safer to give our fate over to parents, teachers, the state, the church, to anyone other than the stranger that is us.

Take back your identity, the unique you that is hiding inside your skin. Life is too precious to give it away to others. It's time to have faith that who you are is much more than who you've been talked into thinking you are. You really are the star you have been looking for your whole life.

Individuality

"Don't be that way,"
     His mother cried,
"Or you will never
     Find a bride."

Say children's parents,
     Teachers, friends.
We're not okay
     Their message sends.

We do our best
     To change our ways,
Make parents proud
     Of who they raise.

Our real self,
     The one inside,
We have to shield,
     We have to hide.

So even we
     Lose who we are,
From bookish nerd
     To superstar.

But why keep dark
     And hide from sight?
We're not some monster
     Who might bite.

We spend our lives
     As who we're not,
Good grades, behave,
     Don't swear a lot.

We live in fear
        That they'll find out.
Perhaps we're just
        Some witless lout.

It's just not so!
        It isn't right!
To hide our self
        From our own sight!

The real you
        Locked deep inside,
Discover there,
        Regain your pride.

You're not some crook
        Nor murderer,
You need no warden,
        Nor deterrerer.

Your genius lies
        In your true self,
The best of you
        Hides on a shelf.

So let it out,
        The real you,
Regain yourself,
        Rejoice! Be true!

Forgive the fools
        Who locked you down.
The Kingdom's yours,
        You wear the crown.

Perfection

Psychologist Wayne Dyer is right in asserting that we are not earthly beings seeking to have a spiritual experience; rather we are spiritual beings having an earthly experience. Perfection is our birthright, our very nature. Our Soul, our Spirit is perfection and we are so much more then just an ego in a body. Our ego has confused Perfection with perfectionism. Perfection is our very nature; perfectionism is nothing more than a cruel hoax, a peccadillo posing as virtue. Perfectionism is petty where Perfection is celestial; perfectionism is limiting while Perfection is freeing; perfectionism is tyranny but Perfection is Godly.

Because we are our own selves and nobody will ever be just like us, we are perfect just as we are. This knowledge will set you free. Free yourself from the yolk of perfectionism and soar to the rapture of your own true Perfection.

Perfection

Perfection is
  The way to go,
It's what I'm told
  And what I know.

Just do things right,
  Make no mistakes,
Perfection rules
  For goodness sakes.

My sums add up,
  My columns straight,
The smallest error
  I do hate.

Both first to work
  And last to leave,
There's no respite
  And no reprieve.

Despite all this
  I don't know how,
Perfection, life
  Will not allow.

A "T" uncrossed,
  Some small miscue,
A color wrong,
  Some fact untrue.

I did my best,
  I really tried,
To claim success
  Would mean I lied.

"And yet," say sages
        Wise and old,
"Your Soul's perfection
        Is foretold."

"And like the God
        From whom you spring,
You proudly wear
        Perfection's ring."

"Perfection-ism
        Is the sin,
That's what you do,
        Not deep within."

For worldly stuff
        Just do your best
In work and play
        And all the rest.

Your body, form, and
        Ego-mind,
You're more than that,
        Another kind.

Perfection's in
        Your Spirit's eye,
It's yours without
        The need to try.

Perfection-ism
        Can't succeed,
Your true Perfection's
        All you need.

Present Moment Living

The present moment is bursting with juicy aliveness.
Really, it's the only place where true, full-dimensional living takes place.
To quote spiritual teacher Leonard Jacobson: "In truth, there is no life
outside of the present moment." Everything but the present is simply
narrative. "This happened yesterday." "That will happen next Tuesday."
We attempt to spice up the past/future with emotion; "I'm so worried
I won't get the job.", "I feel guilty about forgetting to send Tallulah a
Christmas-card." Really, these are all nothing but mental constructs.

Full, three-dimensional living only happens inside of the
precious present. The excitement of living in the actual bloom of life,
the adventure of not knowing what's going to happen, that is what the
present moment brings. Why would we choose not to spend our lives
in the electric reality of the present? Sure, we can learn from the past,
yes, we can plan for the future, but let's live our lives vibrantly within the
present moment.

Present Moment Living

The past was great,
        I've got to say,
The pain and joy
        Of yesterday.

The lessons learned
        Have made me wise,
They've helped me grow
        To my full size.

Those times back then
        I wouldn't miss,
It's fun to sit
        And reminisce.

And up ahead
        My future sits,
Excitement, fears,
        They give me fits.

Will I be rich,
        Or my demise?
It's scary that,
        To fantasize.

I daydream lots
        And worry too,
Despite the fact
        It's all untrue.

Though past is gone
        And future lies,
Still both, my thoughts,
        Monopolize.

What past and future
        Can't avow,
Is true live living
        Here and now.

We're not alive
        Outside the present,
We're flat and dry,
        We're detumescent.

Each moment's precious,
        Filled with joy,
Past-future thoughts
        Cannot employ.

"It's only there,"
        So says my muse,
"You'll find true life
        For you to choose."

She's right, of course,
        We all know that,
To live life now
        Is where it's at.

So, thanks, dear past,
        Now go your way,
And future too,
        You've had your say.

The precious present,
        Now in fashion,
Is my goal
        And my true passion.

If you'd like to order additional copies of

Happy Tymes Rhymes

or its companion volume

Happy 4 Life

please contact **Trafford Publishing**

at

1-888-232-4444

or visit

www.trafford.com